CAPS
FOR SALE

CAPS
FOR SALE

*A Tale of a Peddler, Some Monkeys
and Their Monkey Business*

Told and Illustrated by

Esphyr Slobodkina

HarperCollins*Publishers*

First published by William R. Scott, Inc. as a Young Scott Book.
Copyright 1940 and 1947, © renewed 1968, by Esphyr Slobodkina.
Printed in the U.S.A. All rights reserved.
For information address HarperCollins Children's Books,
a division of HarperCollins Publishers, 10 East 53rd Street, New York, NY 10022
www.harperchildrens.com
Library of Congress Catalog Card Number: 84–43122
ISBN 0–201–09147–X. — ISBN 0–06–025778–4 (lib. bdg.)
ISBN 0–06–443143–6 (pbk.)
09 10 11 12 13 WOR 50

To Rosalind and Emmy Jean,
and to their grandfather
who loved to read to them

Once there was
a peddler who sold caps.
But he was not like
an ordinary peddler
carrying his wares on his back.
He carried them
on top of his head.

First he had on his own
checked cap,
then a bunch of gray caps,
then a bunch of brown caps,
then a bunch of blue caps,
and on the very top
a bunch of red caps.

He walked
up and down the streets,
holding himself very straight
so as not to upset his caps.

As he went along he called,
"Caps! Caps for sale!
Fifty cents a cap!"

One morning
he couldn't sell any caps.
He walked up the street and
he walked down the street calling,
"Caps! Caps for sale. Fifty cents a cap."

But nobody wanted any caps
that morning.
Nobody wanted even a red cap.

He began to feel very hungry,
but he had no money for lunch.

"I think I'll go for a walk in the country,"
said he.
And he walked out of town—
slowly, slowly,
so as not to upset his caps.

He walked for a long time
until he came to a great big tree.

"That's a nice place for a rest,"
thought he.

And he sat down very slowly, under the tree
and leaned back little by little
against the tree-trunk so as not to disturb
the caps on his head.

Then he put up his hand to feel
if they were straight—
first his own checked cap,
then the gray caps,
then the brown caps,
then the blue caps,
then the red caps
on the very top.

They were all there.

So he went to sleep.

He slept for a long time.

When he woke up
he was refreshed
and rested.

But before standing up
he felt with his hand
to make sure his caps were
in the right place.

All he felt was his own
checked cap!

He looked to the right of him.
No caps.

He looked to the left of him.
No caps.

He looked in back of him.
No caps.

He looked behind the tree.
No caps.

Then he looked up into the tree.

And what do you think he saw?

On every branch sat a monkey. On every monkey

was a gray, or a brown, or a blue, or a red cap!

The peddler looked
at the monkeys.

The monkeys looked
at the peddler.

He didn't know
what to do.

Finally he spoke to them.

"You monkeys, you,"
he said,
shaking a finger at them,
"you give me back my caps."

But the monkeys
only shook their fingers
back at him and said,
"Tsz, tsz, tsz."

This made the peddler angry,
so he shook both hands
at them and said,
"You monkeys, you!
You give me back my caps."

But the monkeys only
shook both their hands
back at him and said,
"Tsz, tsz, tsz."

Now he felt quite angry.
He stamped his foot,
and he said,
"You monkeys, you!
You better give me back my caps!"

But the monkeys only
stamped their feet
back at him and said,
"Tsz, tsz, tsz."

By this time
the peddler was really
very, very angry.
He stamped both his feet and
shouted, "You monkeys, you!
You must give me back my caps!"

But the monkeys only
stamped both their feet
back at him and said,
"Tsz, tsz, tsz."

At last he became
so angry that he
pulled off his own cap,
threw it on the ground, and
began to walk away.

But then,
each monkey
pulled off
his cap . . .

and all the gray caps,

and all the brown caps,

and all the blue caps,

and all the red caps

came flying down

out of the tree.

So the peddler
picked up his caps and
put them back on his head—

first his own checked cap,

then the gray caps,

then the brown caps,

then the blue caps,

then the red caps
on the very top.

And slowly, slowly,

he walked back to town calling,

"Caps! Caps for sale!

Fifty cents a cap!"